To Brock, Lauren, Cade,
RyLee, Warrick, Brogan,
and (of course) Bishop,
with love.

Bishop and the Kangaroo

Copyright © 2015 by Jerilyn Tyner

Requests for permission to make copies of any part of the work should be submitted online at info@mascotbooks.com or mailed to Mascot Books, 560 Herndon Parkway #120, Herndon, VA 20170.

PRT0215A

Printed in the United States
Library of Congress Control Number: 2015900911
ISBN-13: 978-1-62086-868-3

www.mascotbooks.com

Bishop
and the
Kangaroo

Jerilyn
Tyner

Illustrations by
Cheryl Crouthamel

"Look at this animal," said Bishop as he showed his picture book to Grandma. "See its great big ears and super-large tail? I think it's a kangaroo."

"You are right!" Grandma agreed. "Kangaroos can jump fast and far. They have a pocket on their bellies to carry their babies in."

"I know. It's called a pouch. I wish I could see a real kangaroo," said Bishop. "Where do they live?"

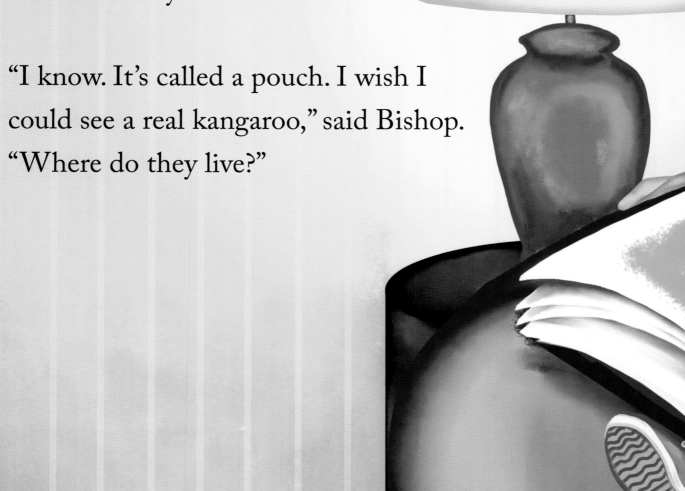

"Hmmm..." Grandma looked thoughtful. "Most kangaroos live in a faraway land called Australia. But I know where there is a kangaroo farm we can visit."

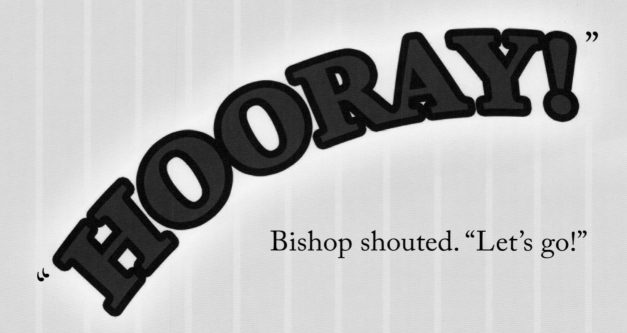

"HOORAY!"

Bishop shouted. "Let's go!"

Bishop put on his favorite green boots. They slid on his feet easy as can be and, quick as a flash, he was ready to go.

It was a short ride to the kangaroo farm. Grandma pointed to a big sign. "Here we are at the Outback Farm. I see the farmer waiting for us by the gate." Bishop hopped out of the car and ran through the gate.

"We came to see the kangaroo," he told the farmer.

"Come along, then." The farmer was wearing boots, too, and Bishop followed him down the path.

Slip. Slosh. Slide. Stomp. Stomp.

There were lots of puddles. Bishop stepped in all of them, but his green boots kept his feet dry.

Some birds with dark feathers strutted along beside them.

Cluck! *Cluck!*

They flapped their wings noisily. Bishop looked at them and said, "You are not kangaroos. You are chickens."

He and Grandma waved their arms.

"SHOO!!!"

The chickens ran away.

Next, they saw some little black and white goats in a pen. Bishop patted one. "You are not a kangaroo, but you are nice."

He picked some dandelions and fed them to the goats. One goat chewed the flowers, but the other goat tried to nibble his boots.

The farmer laughed. "Goats will eat almost anything."

Bishop heard a loud, deep noise.

**Wuh...wuh...
WUUUU!**

It was a tall animal with two legs instead of four. "This is a strange animal," he said to the farmer, "but it is not a kangaroo."

"It's an ostrich, a kind of bird. Watch out for its beak," the farmer told him.

Bishop did not want the ostrich to peck him with its strong beak, so he hurried away, lickety-split! His green boots helped him go fast.

Soon they came to another pen where three animals were resting in the shade. They had great big ears and long, thick tails. The brown one stood up. **Hoppity, hoppity, hop, hop. THUMP.** It came right up to the fence and looked at Bishop.

"A kangaroo! It looks just like the kangaroo in my book," said Bishop.

He could see the kangaroo's pocket, and sure enough, there was a baby peeking out.

The kangaroo sat back, resting on her large hind legs and long, wide tail. She looked at Bishop and blinked her wise eyes as if to say, "Hmmm, so this is a boy."

Suddenly, the kangaroo leapt away.

When Bishop got home, he went

hoppity, hoppity, hop, hop, THUMP

all over the yard. He jumped as far as he could wearing his green rubber boots.

"Watch me jump, Grandma! I have ears and a pocket, like a kangaroo. But I don't have a tail." And off he hopped!

FUN FACTS

This picture of Earth shows the land of Australia. See how big it is? It is surrounded by the ocean. How could you get there? Could you walk in your boots, or would you need a boat or an airplane?

A baby kangaroo is called a joey. When it's born, it is only as big as a lima bean. The joey grows fast in its mother's pouch where it lives for eight more months. Can you show with your hands how big you were when you were born?

The ostrich is the biggest bird in the world, but it cannot fly. It can run very fast, and it can swim fast, too. Ladies used to use ostrich feathers to decorate their hats. If you made a funny hat, what would you use to decorate it?

Goat families have interesting names. The father goat is "Billy," the mother is "Nanny," and their babies are called "kids." Kids like to eat sweet things, like fruit. They even eat the leaves. What is your favorite fruit? Do you think a kid would like to eat it, too?

What good answers you gave! Now, go back through the story and see if you can find the hidden boots in each picture. Have fun!

Jerilyn Tyner is a teacher and freelance writer whose historical novel *The Canterbury Question* was released in 2013 by Desert Breeze Publishing Inc. She has over 50 publishing credits in various categories including professional journals, nonfiction articles, short stories, and poetry. *Bishop and the Kangaroo* is the beginning in a series of adventures based on the author's experiences with her first grandchild.

Jerilyn's lifelong love of language and literature began when she was a preschooler memorizing her favorite Little Golden Books, and continued through a teaching career spanning over two decades. Besides being an enthusiastic devotee of literature, she is a mother of four sons and a grandmother who likes listening to children, seeing the world through their eyes, and telling stories to her "kids."

To enjoy more of her work, go to www.byjerilyn.com.

Have a book idea?

Contact us at:

Mascot Books
560 Herndon Parkway
Suite 120
Herndon, VA 20170

info@mascotbooks.com | www.mascotbooks.com